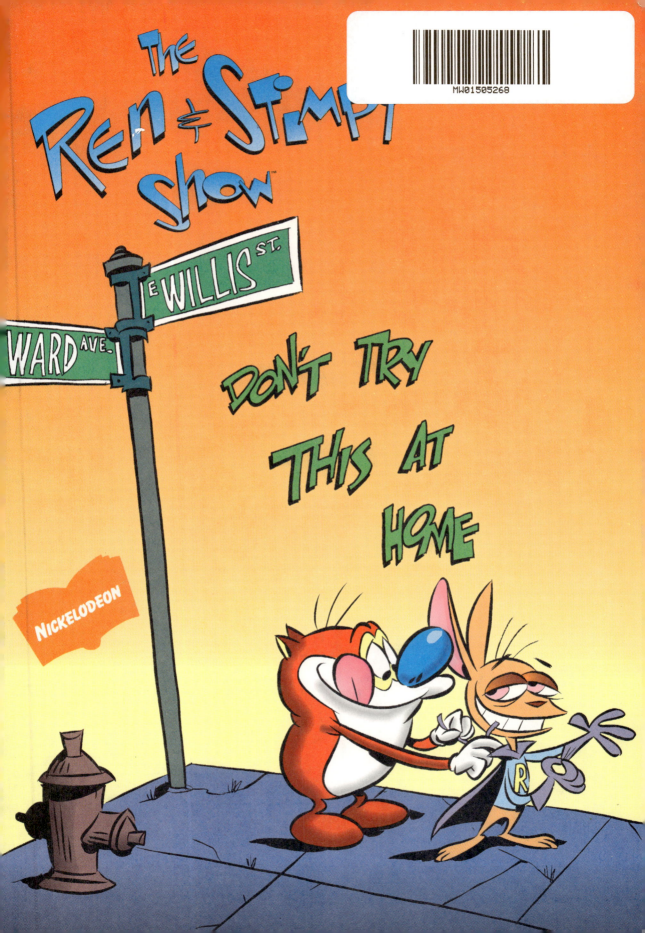

PROUDLY BROUGHT
TO YOU BY:

DAN SLOTT
WRITER
MIKE KAZALEH AND
KEN MITCHRONEY
ARTISTS
BRAD K. JOYCE
LETTERER
ED LAZELLARI
COLORS
MIKE LACKEY
REPRINT EDITOR
FABIAN NICIEZA
ORIGINAL SERIES EDITOR
TOM DeFALCO
EDITOR IN CHIEF

TABLE OF CONTENTS

BUG OUT
5

DESSERT O'RAMA
16

POOL O'FOOLS
17

REN'S PEACEFUL PLACE
27

YOU CAN EAT IT
47

NIGHT OF A THOUSAND EEDIOTS
50

TEACHER BINGO
60

ORGANS OF DOOM
63

WAKKA MAKKA HOËK MEKKA STIMPY HO!
73

TRASH DAY
84

DON'T TRY THIS AT HOME
86

GRAND FINALE
94

CHAPTER 1

DEDICATION:

This one's for Glenda. I'd love you if you were a fish.

DAN

To Sergio Aragonés — A real sweetheart and a d___ fine cartoonist.

M. KAZALEH

ACKNOWLEDGEMENTS:

You've often seen the names of a lot of people who get to do all the fun and glamourous jobs. Obvious people: writer, artists, letterer, colorist, original editor, original assistant editor, reprint editor, editor, and editor in chief. But there are a lot of unsung heroes who help a book like this one get out, people like:

Susan Lopusniak, Will McRobb, Christine Slusarz, Carlos Lopez, Tom Browning, Pete Tirella, Todd Walker, the Marvel Bullpen, Romita's Raiders, the Repro Dept., Dawn Geiger, Tom B. & Manny G., and, of course, all a' youse readers.

Remember guys — we people on the other page love you. Really. That's why our page comes first.

THE REN & STIMPY SHOW™ DON'T TRY THIS AT HOME. Originally published in magazine form as THE REN & STIMPY SHOW #'s 9-12. Published by Marvel Comics. OFFICE OF PUBLICATION: 387 PARK AVENUE SOUTH, NEW YORK, N.Y. 10016. THE REN & STIMPY SHOW (including all prominent characters featured in this issue and the distinctive likenesses thereof) is a trademark owned and licensed for use by NICKELODEON, a programming service of Viacom International, inc., and is used only with permission. All rights reserved. All Ren & Stimpy material Copyright © 1994 Nickelodeon. All rights reserved. All other material Copyright © 1994 Marvel Entertainment Group, Inc. All rights reserved. No part of this book may be printed or reproduced in any manner without the written permission of the publisher. Printed in Canada. ISBN #0-7851-0023-7. First Printing: March, 1994. GST #R127032852   10 9 8 7 6 5 4 3 2 1

RING!
RING!

HELLO?

YES, EET EES WE WHO ARE BUG HUNTERS!

WHAT? YOUR DWELLING EES EENFESTED?

SAY NO MORE! WE'RE ON OUR WAY!

LOAD UP, STIMPY! EET'S TIME ONCE AGAIN TO MAKE THIS LAND SAFE FOR EETS EENSECT-FEARING DENIZENS!

KLUNK!

STIMPSON J. CAT: PROFESSIONAL BUG-HUNTER READY AN' REPORTIN' FOR DUTY, SIR!

DON'T GET COCKY, MEESTER! REMEMBER THE EXTERMEENATOR'S CREDO!

NO MATTER HOW MANY HIGH-TECH GEEZMOS WE HAVE...

...OUR GREATEST WEAPON WEELL EVER BE OUR SHARP WEETS AND OUR KEEN POWERS OF OBSERVATION!

THEY GONE YET?

YEAH!

SLAM!

PHEW, COULDN'T HOLD THAT FER MUCH LONGER!

TELL ME ABOUT IT, PAL!

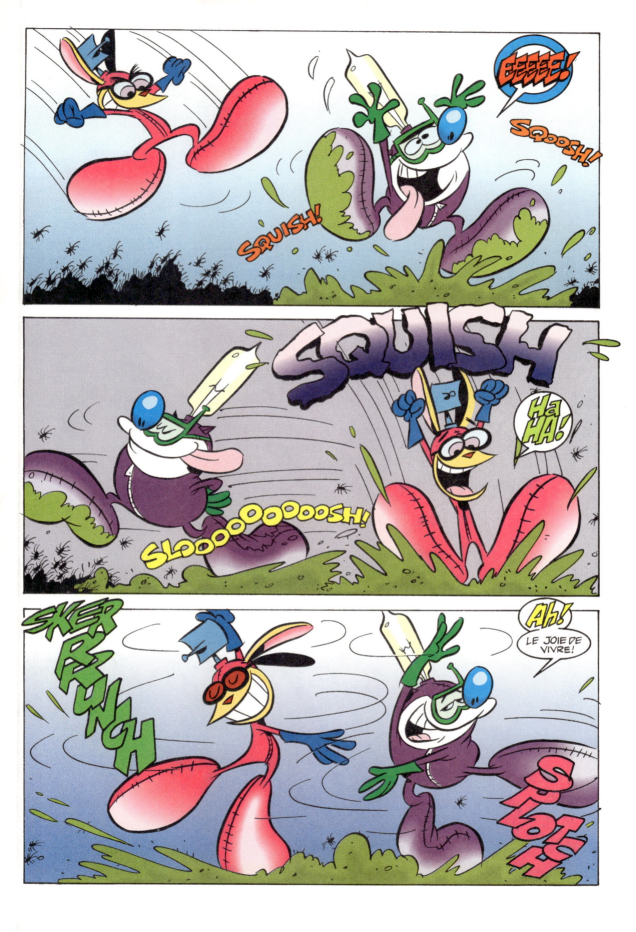

Stimpy's Dessert-O-Rama

HEY KIDS! IF YOU LIKED THAT BIG OL' DINOSAUR FROM THE LAST STORY...

...THEN HAVE *I* GOT A DESSERT FOR YOU: *THE LA BREA TAR PIT SUNDAE!*

ALL YOU NEED IS SOME DIRT-COLORED ICE CREAM (CHOCOLATE, COFFEE, OR MINT-CHIP)--

--GREEN SPRINKLES--

--CHOCOLATE SYRUP--

--AND ANIMAL COOKIES.

IN A DISH OF ICE CREAM, POUR IN HOT FUDGE TO SIMULATE A TAR PIT...

...THEN ADD A RING OF SPRINKLES FOR GRASSY MARSH LAND...

AND FINALLY, LET YOUR ANIMAL COOKIES WALLOW IN THE PRIMORDIAL OOZE...

HEEELP MEEE, I'M SINKING TO MY UNTIMELY DOOOOOOM!

PRETTY FUN, HUH?

BE HERE NEXT TIME WHEN I'LL SHOW YOU HOW TO RE-CREATE THE VOMITORIUMS OF ANCIENT ROME USING ONLY MARZIPAN, RED LICORICE AND MARMALADE!

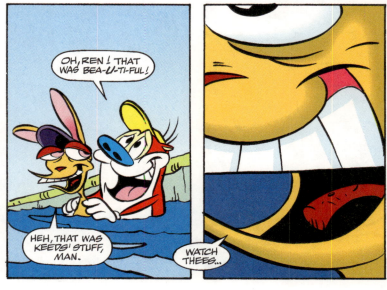

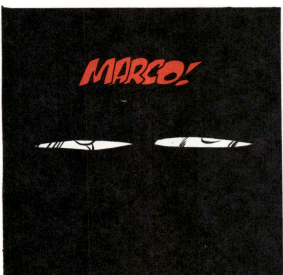

CHAPTER
2

MONKEY.

OSTRICH.

WATUSI.

DYSLEXIC PRETZEL.

INCONTINENT FLAMINGO.

AND FINALLY--SPASMATIC JELLYROLL!

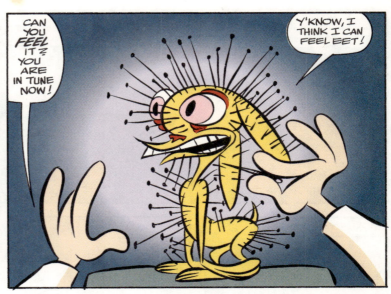

Ahh! HELLO DEAR HOME! I HAVE RETURNED!

VINNI VIDDI VISHI SWAA!

HEY STIMPY, I'M BACK!

SO WHAT HAVE YOU BEEN UP TO, YOU MEESCHEEVIOUS LEETLE SCAMP!

HYAAA!

YOU--YOU--YOU--GOT CHOCOLATE EEN MY PEANUT BUTTER!!

SCHLORK

UNCLE LUMPY'S PEANUT BUTTER

OH, YOU'VE REALLY DONE EET THEES TIME!

UNCLE LUMPY'S PEANUT BUTTER

I'M GONNA-- I'M GONNA-- ≥Fffft shmkk kneh deedeep≤

REN, NO! DON'T LOSE YOUR TEMPER!

REMEMBER WHAT THE DOCTOR SAID.

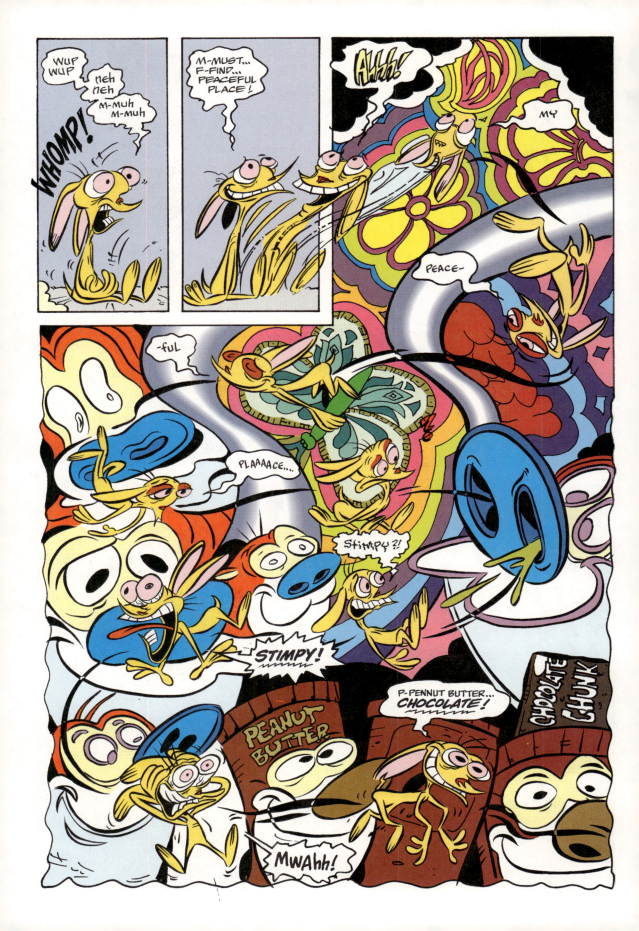

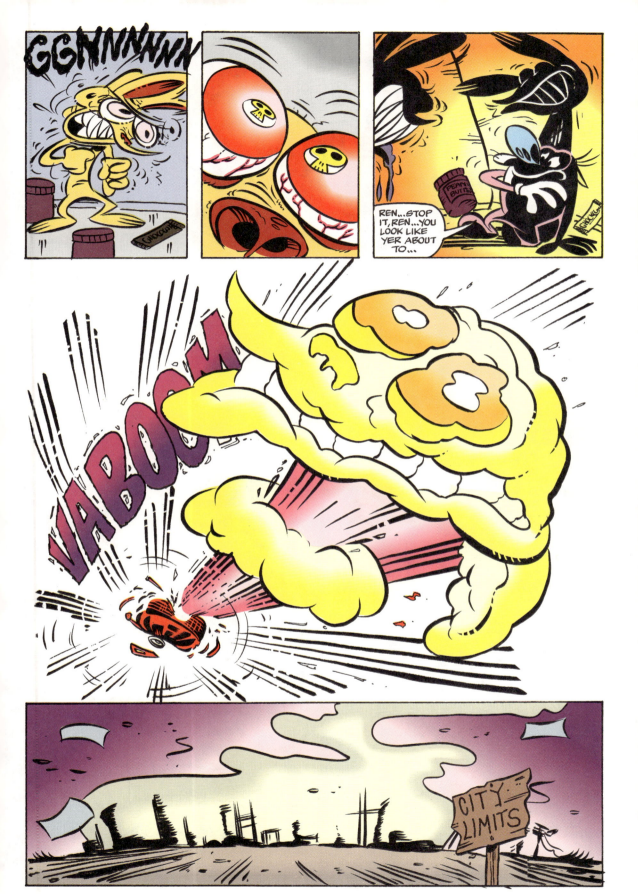

SO WHAT HAPPENED NEXT, GREAT, GREAT, GRAMPA REN? DIDJA *DIE*?

NEH, 'COURSE NOT, YA LEETLE WEEPER-SNAPPER.

Y'SEE EET WAS *THEN* THAT I FOUND MY ONE, *TRUE*, PEACEFUL PLACE.

WELL, THANKS FOR THAT GREAT STORY, *GRAMPA REN*!

ANYTIME, SONNY. NOW YOU RUN ALONG AND PLAY NOW!

SQUEEKY SQUEEKY SQEEKY

EEE!

STIMPY! GET OVER HERE!! *NOW!*

ERR, UHH... WHY *REN*?

'CAUSE WE'RE GOIN' TO VISIT MY PEACEFUL PLACE!

CRACK!

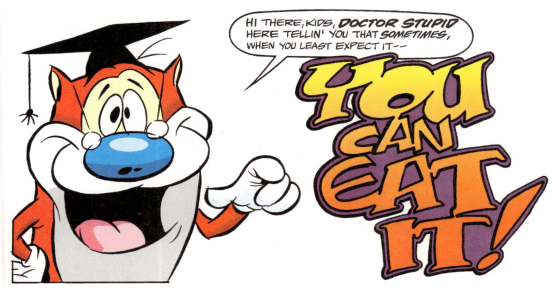

CHAPTER
3

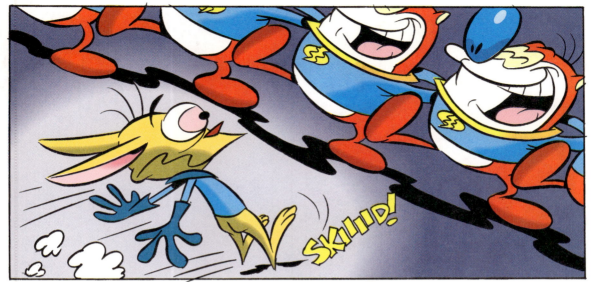

HEY, DUDE, WELCOME TO THE *MEGAVILLE GALLERIA,* THE MOST HUMONGAZOID MALL IN THE WORLD. LIKE SHOUR, Y'KNOW?

I'M *SUZY Q&A,* THE INFORMATION BABE, ANYTHING YOU NEED TO KNOW, I'M YOUR GAL!

INFORMATION

"the *stupid* image." DISPOSABLE INCOME ELIMINATION STATION

N' LET ME TELL YOU, THERE'S A *LOT* TO KNOW ABOUT THIS MALL...

...LOTSA DARK SECRETS LURK BEHIND ITS LINOLEUM-MOSAICED WALLS AND ITS TWO-PLY CARPETING!

FER EXAMPLE--THERE'S THE JR. MISS MYSTIQUE BOUTIQUE...

Teen Fashions by HELLN A HANBASKET

...WHERE THEY SAY THERE'S A LIFE-LIKE MANNEQUIN FOR EVERY MALL GAL WHO COULDN'T PAY HER TAB...

...OR THE *MEGAVILLE MULTIVERSAL CAR PARK...*

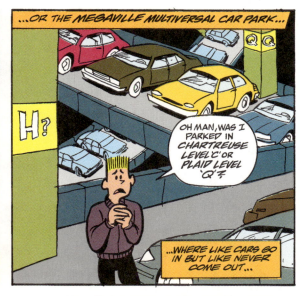

OH MAN, WAS I PARKED IN CHARTREUSE LEVEL 'C' OR PLAID LEVEL 'Q'?

...WHERE LIKE CARS GO IN BUT LIKE NEVER COME OUT...

...OR *LOU'S BIG WORLD O'COMICS,* WHERE YOU CAN BUY A COPY OF JUST ABOUT ANY COMIC...

...BUT DON'T READ THE PANEL ON THE PAGE WE'RE ON NOW--OR YOU COULD GET TRAPPED IN AN *INFINITY VORTEX...*

HEY, KIDS! COMICS!

SPACE ARK

CAPTAIN JACK

HAR★HAR COMICS

GARISH COMICS

...FOREVER READING ABOUT YOURSELF READING ABOUT YOURSELF READING ABOUT...

HEY KID...

FOOMPH!

Say, KIDS! why think?!? INSTEAD PLAY ZNERK A GREAT VIDEO GAME

MEET ZNERK THE JERK!

FROM THE PAGES OF REN & STIMPY #1 IN THEIR FIRST SOLO ADVENTURE!
TANK & BRENNER: MALL COPS!
in THE ORGANS OF DOOM!
DIDN'T ANYONE EVER TELL YOU COMICS ROT YOUR BRAIN?
ALL I CAN SAY IS, IT'S A GOOD THING WE HAVE THESE GUYS LOOKIN' OUT FOR US!
HEY, KIDS! COMICS!
ALF, BILL & TED
TALES OF MAO
FRAP MAN
SKIP DEEZ LOVE MACHINE
714
EGRET COMICS
CHOO CHOO MAGOO!
BASIL & OREGANO!
KATO!
WHAT?!?
YARN MAN
SPLORG!
TUNGA the CAVE-BOY
CAPTAIN CAHUENGA
ANT FUNNIES
APE HIJINX
the SALAD DAYS of REGINALD TWIT
ROCK 'N' ROLL DIETY!
25¢

HEY, T&B, WHUZZUP?

HEY, THERE, SUZE! WE'RE LEARNING ESPERANTO, THE INTERNATIONAL LANGUAGE!

MY STRUDEL'S IN YOUR OVEN. ¡MI ESTRÜDLEADO ICH TU MICROWAYUV!

THE BIG INTERNATIONAL MALL COP CONVENTION'S COMING UP, BUT WE'RE NOT SURE WHICH COUNTRY IT'S IN THIS YEAR.

IN FACT, WE'RE PRETTY SURE WE'RE GONNA MAKE MALL COPS OF THE YEAR THIS TIME!

BUT KNOWIN' ESPERANTO, WE'LL BE PREPARED.

BUT DIDN'T YOU DUDES LET TWO MALL PERPS GET AWAY LAST YEAR?*

*SEE REN & STIMPY #1.--FABE

FOR THE LUVVA MIKE, SUZE! YOU KNOW WHAT IT'S LIKE TO BE A MALL COP AND HAVE TO LIVE WITH SOMETHING LIKE THAT?

HUNH?! DO YOU?!

C'MON PAL, LET'S GO TO THE FOOD COURT.

F-F-FOOD OF ALL NATIONS?

YEAH.

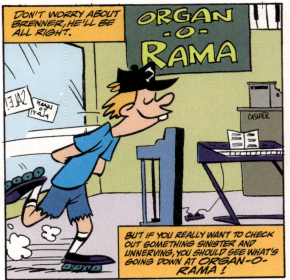

TOTALLY OBLIVIOUSO TO THE HORROR ENSUING ON THE LEVELS ABOVE, T&B TAKE IN THE SPLENDORS OF THE FAB FOOD COURT...

Chèz EGGROTT

FALAFEL BOUTIQUE

KREPLACH KORNER

RIGATONI R' TUBS

¿DONDE ESTA MI HUEVOS RANCHEROS?*

¡AQUI, EN MI PANTALONES!**

*TRANSLATION: "WHY IS YOUR HEEL GRINDING INTO MY SHIN?"

**"YOU DESERVE NO LESS, FOREIGN-DEVIL!"

WITHOUT WARNING, THE AIR ERUPTS IN A BLOOD-CURDLING RUMBA-BEAT!

WHO CAN BLAME THE MALL GALS AND GUYS FOR RUNNING IN ABSOLUTE

FREAKISH TERROR!

CRASH!

VO PUTTEN DAS "BOOP" EN DER "BOOP BOOP SHA DOOP"?*

DEINE MUTTER.**

*"WHY DOES MY BODY FEEL SO STRANGE AND TINGLY?"

**"YOU ATE MANY PRUNES, I GATHER."

AND IN THE INFINITE GARAGE OF THE *MULTIVERSAL CAR PARK*, THOSE ORGANS HAVE BEEN TRAPPED IN AN ENDLESS CONGA-LINE TO THIS DAY!!

THEIR MUFFLED CRIES, DEEP IN THE BOWELS OF *INDIGO LEVEL 8*, WAFT UP THROUGH THE AIR DUCTS AND COME OUT THE MALL'S VENTS.

ONE OLD TALL MALL TALE HAS IT, THAT THAT'S WHERE MALL MUSAK COMES FROM.

ASK ME, N' I'LL TELL YA IT'S THE *GOSH-HONEST TRUTH!* AND WE OWE IT ALL TO THOSE TWO BRAVE SOULS--*TANK & BRENNER:*

MALL COPS!

IAY EAR-HAY ARVEL-MAY OMICS-CAY IRED-FAY CIR-THAY ANSLATOR-TRAY!

A-HAY! A-HAY!

NASAL EMPORIUM

STUFF QUE

CARTOON RIPOFF

FORKS "R" US

"GASTRIC BLOCKAGE"

WEIRD STUFF, LADY.

CIAO!

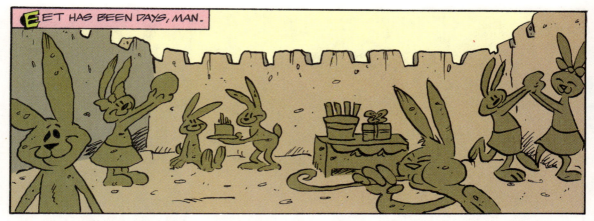

EET HAS BEEN DAYS, MAN.

AND ALL WE'VE HAD TO EAT...

EEE!

SCOOP

...EES STIMPY'S STEENKY LEETER.

Ahh

:Pat Pat:

STIMPY

THE SCARY THEENG EES...

:Gu-hulp:

STIMPY

...THE LEETER LEVEL DOESN'T SEEM TO GO DOWN.

AND WITH HIS ORGANS A' WILDLY PUMPIN', HE'S FILLED WITH THE STRENGTH OF TEN ASTHMA-HOUND CHIHUAHUAS!*

"Gnuh"

*OR ½ A GERMAN SHEPHERD.—FABE

SNAP

WHAT VIRILITY!

WHAT DEXTERITY!

SNAG!

WHAT A DOG!

HE CAN DO NO WRONG!

FLIP FLIP FLIP

Eh?

Flip Flip Flip Flip Flip

CUT!

SORRY, 'BOUT THAT MR. HO×K. WE'LL SET UP THE SCREEN AGAIN...

'BET THEES KINDA @×☆×!! NEVER HAPPENED TO @×*×!! FRANKIE N' ANETTE!

"EVERYTHING I SAW TOLD ME THAT STIMPSON HAD GONE EENSANE...

KEEP OFF THE MUD

"EET WAS TIME FOR HEEM TO TAKE A LONG TREEP, YES?

"AND I...

"I'D BE HEES PEPPY TOUR GUIDE, SKEEPY!"

I EXPECTED ONE LIKE YOU.

ARE YOU AN ASSASSIN?

A SOLDIER?

I'M NEITHER.

I'M AN ERRAND BOY...

SENT BY THE GROCERY CLERKS...

TO COLLECT THE BEELL!

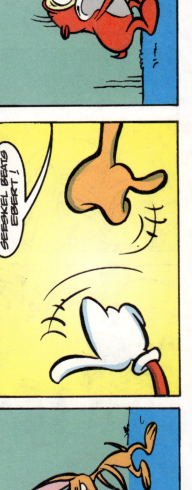

DON'TCHA GET EET? WE'RE TRAINED PROFESSIONALS!
SO WHEN YOU SEE US DOIN' SOMETHING EEN THE COMEECS...
DON'T TRY EET AT HOME!
A SPECIAL SERVICE ANNOUNCEMENT BROUGHT TO YOU BY
MARVEL COMICS AND NICKELODEON

FOR EENSTANCE, YOU REMEMBER EEN OUR STORY "BUG OUT..."

...WHEN STIMPSON AND I CRUSHED UP BUGS...

...AND SOLD THE BUG JUICE AS A REFRESHING SOFT DRINK?

Bug Juice 5¢

WELL, EEF YOU AND YOUR FRIENDS DEED THAT...

SPWOSH

SPWISH

HOLD IT RIGHT THERE, PUNKS!

USFDA! YOU'RE BUSTED!

YOU'D GET ARRESTED BY THE UNITED STATES FOOD AND DRUG ADMINISTRATION...

PADDY WAGON

...AND SPEND NUMEROUS YEARS EEN THE BEEG HOUSE!

HERE'S A SCENE FROM "NIGHT OF A THOUSAND EEDIOTS," WHERE I PULLED OUT MY TONGUE AND REPEATEDLY HIT IT WITH A HAMMER.

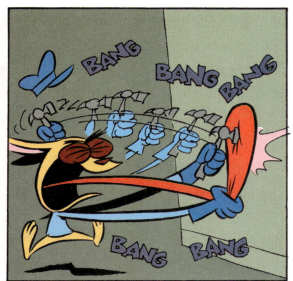

BANG BANG BANG BANG BANG

AND HERE'S WHAT WOULD HAPPENED EEF YOU TRIED TO DO THAT...

HUH?

GNNNN.!!

FLOOMP!

AND WHAT ABOUT THAT SCENE FROM "TEACHER BINGO," WHERE STIMPY BLEW HIS BRAIN THROUGH HIS NOSE?

Hello. I am Mrs. Fitzgerald. today's lesson: The spleen and its place in history.

Snurk!

BOINK!

NOW UNDER NO CIRCUMSTANCES SHOULD THEES BE ATTEMPTED WEETH A NORMAL NOSE AND BRAIN!

WAR IS PEACE

$2+2=5$

$6 \times 7 = 8$

AHHHHH!

FOUR LEGS GOOD

TWO LEGS BAD

AND FINALLY, AND MOST IMPORTANTLY, REMEMBER **THIS** SCENE FROM "WAKKA MAKKA HOÉK, MEKKA STIMPY HO?"

HERE STIMPSON AND MYSELF EAT CHERRY FLAVORED PIZ...

PIZ

AND HERE'S WHAT HAPPENS IF YOU EAT PIZ...

BOOM!

SO, EEN CLOSING... **DON'T DO ANYTHING** YOU SEE US DO EEN OUR COMICS!

...AND WHEN IN DOUBT, USE YOUR BRAIN!

I KNOBE I WIBSH I DIB!

END

FLUMP!

=WHEW!=

KA-BLOOEY!

--TODAY ONLY--
the INCREDIBLE HOËK!
WATCH as he DIVES
SIXTY STORIES
into a RIGHT SOCK!
(KIDS, DON'T TRY THIS AT HOME!)

RIGHT
SOCK.

ONLY.. HOËK!

·ENDSVILLE·